My dear mouse friends,

Have I ever told you how much I love science fiction? I've always wanted to write incredible adventures set in another dimension, but I've never believed that parallel universes exist . . . until now!

That's because my good friend Professor Paws von Volt, the brilliant, secretive scientist, has just made an incredible discovery. Thanks to some mousetropic calculations, he determined that there are many different dimensions in time and space, where anything could be possible.

The professor's work inspired me to write this science fiction adventure in which my family and I travel through space in search of new worlds. We're a fabumouse crew: the spacemice!

I hope you enjoy this intergalactic adv

Geron

PROFESSOR
WS VON VOLT

THE SPACEMICE

GERONIMO STILTONIX

TRAP STILTONIX

THEA STILTONIX

GRANDFATHER WILLIAM STILTONIX

ROBOTIX

BENJAMIN STILTONIX AND BUGSY WUGSY

Geronimo Stilton

SPACEMICE

THE GALACTIC GOAL

Scholastic Inc.

ISBN 978-0-545-74620-5

Based on an original idea by Elisabetta Dami.

www.geronimostilton.com

Published by Scholastic Inc., 557 Broadway, New York, NY 10012.

Text by Geronimo Stilton
Original title *Sfida galattica all'ultimo gol*
Cover by Flavio Ferron
Interior illustrations by Giuseppe Facciotto (design)
and Daniele Verzini (color)
Graphics by Chiara Cebraro

Special thanks to Shannon Penney
Translated by Julia Heim
Interior design by Kevin Callahan / BNGO Books

12 11 10 9 8 7 6 5 4 3 2 1   15 16 17 18 19 20/0

Printed in the U.S.A.   40
First printing, 2015

In the darkness of the farthest galaxy in time and space is a spaceship inhabited exclusively by mice.

This fabumouse vessel is called the **MouseStar 1**, and I am its captain!

I am Geronimo Stiltonix, a somewhat accident-prone mouse who (to tell you the truth) would rather be writing novels than steering a spaceship.

But for now, my adventurous family and I are busy traveling around the universe on exciting intergalactic missions.

THIS IS THE LATEST ADVENTURE OF THE SPACEMICE!

Incoming Video Message!

It was a **calm** Monday morning, and I had just started eating a cosmic cheese Danish in my cabin. The onboard computer opened my daily **news** summary. A ship's captain has to be informed about what's going on across the **UNIVERSE**, after all!

Oh, excuse me— I haven't introduced myself! My name is Stiltonix, **Geronimo Stiltonix**. I am the captain of the

MOUSESTAR 1, home of the spacemice!

As I was saying, I read the titles of the articles in **SPACE NEWS**: *Firemaker Volcano Erupts; Asteroids Pass Through Galaxies 88532 and 22398; Spacecraft Crashes Near Antarex Constellation; Soccerix Championship to Begin Next Week on Planet Athletica.*

Oh, sports!

I have to admit, I'm not a very SPORTY mouse. Just the thought

of going for a *RUN* makes my legs turn softer and **floppier** than Martian mozzarella!

No, I'm no athlete — my dream is to become a great WRITER. I have been trying to finish writing my book, *The Amazing Adventures of the Spacemice*, for ages, but I never manage to do it because some sort of galactic trouble always pops up!

That Monday, luckily, everything seemed calm . . . until an alarm went off, making me **jump** to my paws in fright.

Hologramix, the onboard computer, suddenly MATERIALIZED in front of me.

"INCOMING VIDEO MESSAGE! INCOMING VIDEO MESSAGE! INCOMING VIDEO MESSAGE!"

I looked down sadly at my **half-full** mozzarella smoothie and my **UNFINISHED** cosmic cheese Danish. I sighed. "Can't I look at the message later?"

"**Impossible!**" Hologramix cried. "It requires an immediate response!"

I protested. "But I still need to finish my **BREAKFAST** . . ."

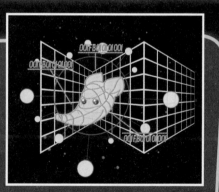

HOLOGRAMIX
MouseStar I's onboard computer

Species: Ultra-advanced artificial intelligence
Specialty: Controls all functions of the spaceship, including the autopilot function
Characteristics: Considers itself to be indispensable
Defining Features: Appears wherever and whenever it's needed

"Negative, Captain. You must respond **immediately**!" Hologramix replied firmly.

Stellar Swiss slices, I couldn't win this argument. "*All right, all right!* Let's hear it."

A captain's work is never done!

An Unexpected Invitation

HOLOGRAMIX began to explain, "Captain, we received a video message from planet Athletica of the **SPORTIVIUM** constellation. Its location is distant from ours, according to protonic velocity and converting the distance in photonic quantifiers . . ."

I didn't understand a lunar cheese crumb of what Hologramix was saying! "Can I just watch the MESSAGE?" I said. "You can explain the details to me later."

On the **SCREEN** in my cabin, the image of an **ALIEN** holding a ball appeared, and the video message began.

Galactic greetings!

"Galactic greetings, Captain Stiltonix. My name is Diego Goalor, and I am the president of the **Intergalactic Federation of Soccerix**. I'm sure you know that our **PLANET** holds an Intergalactic Soccerix Championship every four cosmic years . . ."

Soccerix championship?

It sounded familiar . . . Oh, that's right! I had just read about it in the news!

The **MESSAGE** continued, "Every time we organize the tournament, we select eight cosmic populations to compete against one another for the *Great Intergalactic Cup*! I am formally inviting the spacemice team to participate in the twelfth **soccerix championship**, which will take place in two weeks. We ask you, honorable spacemice, to please confirm your participation. **SINCEREST STELLAR SALUTATIONS!**"

The video message closed with a beep, and I stared at the blank screen, **CONFUSED**.

The spacemice soccerix team? I shook my snout.

What did I know about **SOCCERIX**?

I would just have to tell Diego Goalor the truth: We spacemice did not have a soccerix team. We didn't even know the **RULES** of the game!

I tried to respond to the video message, but I couldn't find the right button. **Sally de Wrench**, the ship's mechanic, had updated all the **MONITORS** in the cabins. The new command center was full of markings that I couldn't understand. Crusty space cheese, how frustrating!

I finally found what I thought was the right button. I pressed it, and . . . nothing happened.

So I tried another button, and . . . **nothing**!

I made one last try, but . . . nothing!

I took a deep breath. Surely someone in the **control room** could help me!

You Don't Know How to Play Soccerix?!

As I entered the control room, my dear nephew **BENJAMIN** ran enthusiastically toward me.

"Hooray, Uncle Geronimo!" he cried. "The spacemice are going to play in the soccerix championship! What mouserific news!"

Black holey cheese! "B-b-but how do you know that?" I stammered in surprise.

He grinned. "Because of the message you sent to everyone!"

OH NO! When I was trying to respond to the video message and thought nothing was happening, had I accidentally forwarded it to **ALL** the spacemice? **WHAT A MESS!**

Benjamin tugged on my paw. "Uncle, my uniform is all ready to go! I can be part of the **TEAM**, right?"

I was about to point out that we didn't have a team when Bugsy Wugsy, Benjamin's friend, **caught up** with us.

"I want to play, too! Benjamin and I are a stellar **PAIR**!" she exclaimed.

Looking into their excited **EYES**, I felt myself melt like a big bowl of solar smoked Gouda ice cream. I'm such a **SOFTY**!

So I sighed and said, "Of course you can be on our team."

Benjamin and Bugsy hugged me gleefully.

"Uncle Geronimo, you're the best uncle in the whole **galaxy**!" Benjamin cried. "You'll be the team captain, right?"

I smiled. "Oh, Benjamin, I'll come with you, but I **won't** be playing on the tea—"

SUDDENLY, the door to the control room opened again, and a deep voice thundered, "Of course you will be part of the team, Grandson!"

Mousey meteorites, Grandfather William Stiltonix had arrived!

"**H-h-hi, Grandfather!**" I stammered. "So you got the . . . umm, the invite, too?"

"Of course I got it!" he hollered. "And I bothered **COMING** all the way here to find out how the team is shaping up! You don't think you're going to get out of playing, right? The **Intergalactic Soccerix**

Championship is extremely important!"
He waved his paws for emphasis. "And
the captain—which is, unfortunately,
you—*must* play. The **REPUTATION** of
all the spacemice is at stake!"

I stammered, "Y-yes, it is an h-honor,
b-but I —"

Grandfather shook his head. "Don't tell
me that **YOU DON'T KNOW
HOW TO PLAY** soccerix!"

Gulp!

You cosmic cheesebrain!

I hesitated, but then admitted, "Um, yes . . . that's right . . ."

Grandfather snorted. "I knew it, **YOU COSMIC CHEESEBRAIN**! Well, never mind that. You have two weeks to **LEARN**!"

Grandfather held his snout in the air and said proudly, "When I was your age, I was a soccerix champion! And that's why I will be . . . THE TEAM COACH!"

Grandfather William, our coach? I was squeakless. That was possibly the worst news I had ever heard—almost as bad as that time the **MOUSESTAR 1** had run out of cheese!*

"Study the soccerix rules, Captain Cheddarbreath!" Grandfather said firmly. "I've already loaded them onto your computer."

*Read all about that in my book *You're Mine, Captain!*

SOCCERIX

Soccerix is a game in which players try to kick a ball into the opposing team's goal. The sport is played in teams of seven: one goalie, two defenders, two midfielders, and two forwards (though the players' roles can change around, depending on what's happening in the game).

Here's what the playing field looks like:

Glowing lines to mark the borders of the field

Laser goals

Laser cameras to capture fouls and illegal plays

Super-Turbo Spot:
If the ball is kicked on the red dot, it activates a special super-turbo button—the ball can't be stopped, and the player scores a surefire galactic goal!

Robot-Ref:
This referee has 360-degree laser vision, which allows it to monitor the entire playing field.

PLAYERS WANTED!

The next **morning**, a strange voice woke me in the middle of my favorite DREAM — the one where I am in the largest **bookstore** in the galaxy, autographing copies of my new novel. Leaping light-years, I REALLY wanted to be a writer!

Half-asleep, I opened the door of my cabin to see who was there. But instead of one mouse, I was greeted by a *LOOOOONG LINE* of rodents who lived on *MouseStar 1*!

I shook my snout to clear my head. Had they ACTUALLY come for signed copies of my book? I hadn't even finished the first chapter yet!

Confused, I quietly asked my personal assistant robot, "**Assistatrix**, what are all those mice doing out there?"

In his **METALLIC** voice, Assistatrix responded, "They are all here for the **soccerix** team tryouts, Captain."

Meteoric mozzarella!

"**TRYOUTS?!**" I yelped. "What tryouts?"

Just then, I noticed that the hallway outside my cabin was lit up with enormouse

ARROWS and SIGNS about the team selection. My mouth fell open. Who could have put them there?

Suddenly, a snout that I knew well poked out of the crowd. It was my cousin **Trap Stiltonix**!

"**Hi, cuz!**" He snickered at the look of shock on my snout. "Did you see how many fabumouse candidates we have here? **Picking** the players is going to be a blast!"

Rat-munching robots! I should have known that this was all Trap's doing!

"Um, yes, **there sure are a lot of them**," I squeaked. "Too bad that I have so much to do in the control room today—you know, captain stuff . . ."

He smirked. "The only work you're doing today is as **TEAM CAPTAIN**! Grandfather William ordered Thea to take over command of the ship for you. He was the one who told me to organize the **TRYOUTS**, too. If we had waited for you to do it, we wouldn't be ready for **LIGHT-YEARS**!"

Before I could even squeak, Trap patted me on the back. "**CHEER UP, GERRYKINS!** Finally, you're going to have a little fun instead of staying holed up writing that long, boring **BOOK** of yours."

What could I do? Resigned, I followed

Trap and the hopeful soccerix players to the *MouseStar 1*'s TECHNOGYM. We started by selecting the goalie and the center fielders. It took two astrohours, but in the end we chose TIM WHISKERKICKS as the goalie and the TAILTWISTER twins — David and *Alex* — as midfielders.

The forwards lined up to take some shots toward the goal.

What a cosmic disaster!

Take that!

The whole thing ended with:

1. a plasma screen in **SHATTERS**.

2. a ball **LAUNCHED** into the galaxy.

3. another ball **FLYING** into my snout!

Trap frowned. "No, this is no good. There's only one solution."

A **CHILL** ran down my tail. What fur-brained plan did my cousin have in mind?

Trap announced, "We need some *Dog Star fondue*! With full stomachs, we'll be able to judge the players better."

I breathed a **SIGH** of relief as we headed to the Space Yum Café. Food was a good idea.

SQUIZZY, our onboard cook, greeted us happily. "Hello! I've prepared a menu rich in protein for you—**BOILED BLUE ALGAE!**"—

YUCK! We protested, "But we want fondue!"

Squizzy looked at us sharply. "No, you need to nourish yourselves like athletes—under **ORDERS** from your coach, William Stiltonix!"

For you—boiled blue algae!

START, SPRINT, SHOOT!

The next morning was our first **TEAM** practice. We hadn't found any alternate players yet, but at least there were seven of us to start with—me, Trap, Bugsy, Benjamin, *Whiskerkicks*, and the *Tailtwister* twins!

I woke up, ready as I would ever be to head to the **technogym**. Assistatrix handed me my clothes, but something was wrong!

"This isn't my **GYM OUTFIT**," I said, shaking my snout.

"This is your soccerix uniform, Captain," **Assistatrix** explained. "An astrotaxi is waiting to take you to the practice field. You're already **late**!"

With that, Assistatrix grabbed me by the tail and dragged me to the **ASTROTAXI**. I was off!

Out on the field, my teammates were already *RUNNING LAPS* to warm up. Sally de Wrench was there, too. She'd offered to be an alternate player, since she was too busy with her regular work to

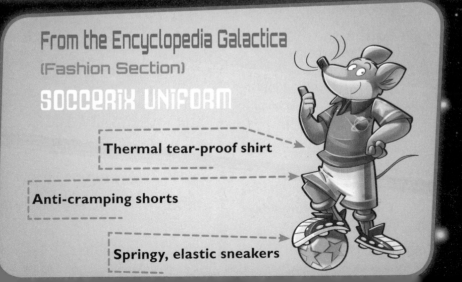

From the Encyclopedia Galactica
(Fashion Section)
SOCCERIX UNIFORM

Thermal tear-proof shirt

Anti-cramping shorts

Springy, elastic sneakers

play full-time. I **GAWKED** at her in admiration—holey craters, what a multitalented mouse!

Before I could squeak, a **METALLIC VOICE** startled me. "Captain, you're late! Start running! **SPRINT, SPRINT, SPRINT!**"

I spun around. "Robotix! What are you doing here?"

"He's my **assistant**, you cosmic cheesebrain!" my grandfather boomed. "Now don't waste another moment. Just follow the orders. **SPRINT, SPRINT, SPRINT!**"

I ran up behind the others. By the time I finished **ONE LAP** around the field, my legs were

TEAM FORMATION

Geronimo Stiltonix (defender)
Trap Stiltonix (defender)
Benjamin Stiltonix (forward)
Bugsy Wugsy (forward)
David Tailtwister (midfielder)
Alex Tailtwister (midfielder)
Tim Whiskerkicks (goalie)
Sally de Wrench (alternate)

as wobbly as a stick of Martian mozzarella.

Oh, for the love of cheese. I still had to do **jumps, sprints, push-ups** . . . and then actually play some soccerix!

After a while, Robotix announced, "Now it is time to try some passes and try shooting at the goal."

Huff, huff . . .

Come on! Move it!

After my many **awkward** attempts to kick the ball, Benjamin came over and showed me what to do. I tried a big **KICK**—I absolutely did **NOT** want to let my nephew down! And this time, I managed to ᴄᴏɴɴᴇᴄᴛ my foot with the ball . . . but it sailed right over the goal and out of bounds. Rats!

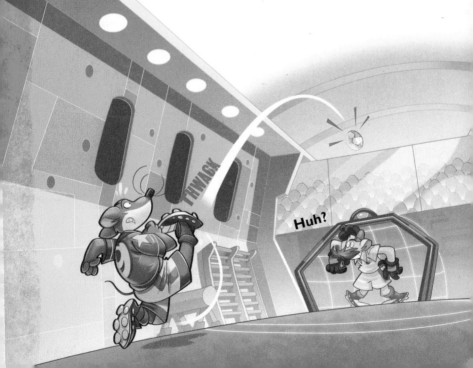

A Stellar Soccerix Player

Benjamin clapped his paws and cheered. "Good job, Uncle! You **kicked it** that time!"

"But now I have to go find the ball!" Robotix grumbled.

Before he could move, the ball appeared again, lit up bright and fiery red. It sailed back over the field—and headed STRAIGHT into the goal!

"**COSMIC CHEDDAR!**" I exclaimed. "Who kicked that incredible shot?"

Benjamin squeaked, "It was a **galactic goal**!"

"A galactic . . . what?" I asked.

"There's a **special spot** on the ball," Benjamin explained. "If you kick that spot, it doubles in speed and **POWER** — you get a surefire goal! But only **true champions** can do it."

While Benjamin was explaining, a little mouse appeared on the sideline. He grinned and waved his paw.

"Hey! What's your name?" Trap asked.

The little mouse answered, "**LIONEL**. Lionel Ratessi."

"And I'm Penny, his mom," said a rodent, walking up behind the young mouse.

Trap shook her paw enthusiastically.

"Based on that GALACTIC GOAL we just saw, your son seems to be an out-of-this-world soccerix player!"

Penny gave a small smile. "Yes, he's GOOD with a ball. It's a shame he isn't quite as good at school!" She LOOKED at Lionel reproachfully.

GRANDFATHER WILLIAM walked up and asked, "Ma'am, would you let your son KICK the ball with us for a bit?"

Be good!

"No, we were just going—" Penny began.

Yes, Mom!

But then Lionel jumped in, begging, "Please, Mom? Just a few kicks!"

"Oh, all right!" his mother said with a sigh.

32

"I'm going to buy some spare parts for our shine-all robot, but as soon as I come back, we're heading home." She waved and walked away.

With a huge grin, Lionel grabbed the ball and showed off his SKILLS.

"Lionel, you're really a fabumouse player!" said Grandfather William, watching in awe.

The time flew by, but soon Penny came back to get Lionel.

Grandfather walked up to Lionel's mother and said, "We would like your son to officially join the SPACEMICE SOCCERIX TEAM. We're preparing for the championship, and he's the all-star forward we were missing!"

Penny frowned and crossed her arms. "I'm sorry, but I'm afraid not. Lionel needs to do his **ROBOTICS*** homework."

As they were walking away, I suddenly had a STELLAR IDEA! "Penny, wait!" I called. "Let Lionel play with us, and I promise that when we get back, he can do an accelerated robotics course with SALLY DE WRENCH, our official onboard technician."

Penny narrowed her eyes. "Hmmm. Is Miss de Wrench experienced?"

"She is the most **experienced** on the spaceship—I mean, in all the galaxy—no, in the whole universe!" I said confidently.

"Well, in that case . . ." Penny said with a small smile. "All right."

---

* Robotics is a subject exploring how to create and program robots.

TIME TO
BLAST OFF!

We practiced all day, every day for twelve days. *It was astronomically tiring!*

But now we seemed almost like a real team, even if Grandfather William still **HOLLERED** at me every once in a while because of my silly mistakes. Luckily, we had Lionel, who always stunned us with his **CHAMPION-CALIBER** kicks!

The day we were leaving for the tournament, Thea arrived to transport us to the planet **ATHLETICA** in her little space pod. The whole team was there, including *MouseStar 1*'s cook, **SQUIZZY**! Huh?

"You're coming, too?" I asked him.

"Of course!" Squizzy said. "You're going to need my boiled algae. After all, a balanced diet is essential for any self-respecting athlete!"

I was about to go COSMIC, but Trap whispered in my ear. "Don't WORRY, Gerry Berry. My bag is stuffed with aged cheeses!"

Whew!

Speaking of bags . . . where was mine, the one with all my CLOTHES in it?

"Holey craters, I forgot my bag! We can't leave yet!" I yelled.

Grandfather William shot me a PIERCING glare. "If you weren't the team captain, I would leave you behind!"

I turned to scurry to my cabin, but just then Assistatrix arrived in a hurry with my bag. BAM!

We ran into each other head-on! My bag flew into the air—and the stuff inside went **EVERYWHERE**! Everyone saw my matching cheese-patterned **pajamas** and my lucky YELLOW SOCKS.

OH, FOR ALL OF SATURN'S RINGS, WHAT A FOOL I MADE OF MYSELF!

BAM

Help!

LET THE GAMES BEGIN!

"Look! There's **ATHLETICA**!" Benjamin announced, pointing out the window of Thea's ship.

I peeked out and saw a planet that looked a lot like . . . a soccerix ball!

I had just begun to consult the *Encyclopedia Galactica* to find out more about the SEPTIMALS, the inhabitants of Athletica, when a squawking voice came out of the spaceship communicator: **"Welcome, spacemice!**

From the Encyclopedia Galactica

THE SEPTIMALS

These are the inhabitants of the planet Athletica. They are historic soccerix champions! They often win, thanks to their blender technique: By swirling their seven legs, they are able to kick the ball incredibly far and fast. They even train with seven balls at the same time!

You can land in area 158!"

"**Message received!**" Thea responded. Turning to us, she said, "Fasten your seat belts—we're about to land!"

A few moments later, the space pod touched down on Athletica, and we all **DISEMBARKED**. We waved to Thea—she was heading back to pilot the *MouseStar 1* while I was gone.

When we turned around, a delegation of

SEPTIMALS with welcome banners were waiting for us!

The septimal who had sent us the video message two weeks earlier walked up to me. "In the name of the septimals, I welcome you to Athletica. We are so HAPPY that you accepted our invitation!"

He kindly directed us to our hotel so we could settle in. On the way, Sally de Wrench was SHOVED by a large, green, and very unfriendly alien. He didn't even apologize!

How RUDE! I had to say something.

Gathering my courage, I approached the alien and said, "Excuse

Let me through!

Ouch!

BANG

me, but you owe Miss de Wrench an apology!"

He peered at me seriously—and then laughed in my face! I almost fainted because his breath was so galactically **stinky**.

Then he hissed, "The **ZOMBORGS** don't ever apologize. Remember that, rat!" He turned around and left without another word. Cosmic cheese balls, how awful!

Once I regained my senses, **Robotix** explained, "Those are the zomborgs, Captain. They are another team that will participate in the soccerix tournament. Unfortunately, they are very hard to beat!"

"Especially if they **breathe** in your face," Trap muttered, chuckling and waving a paw in front of his snout.

But I didn't feel like laughing. Those aliens seemed **VERY DANGEROUS**!

Lost in thought, I didn't even notice that we had arrived at our hotel. Grandfather William decided how we would divide up the rooms. I ended up sharing a room with Trap—who was famouse among the spacemice for his galactic snoring!

From the Encyclopedia Galactica

THE ZOMBORGS

These are the inhabitants of the planet Penaltex, famouse for their aggressive behavior and rudeness. On the soccerix field, they are feared for being relentless rule breakers.

Spacemice Take the Field!

After a sleepless **NIGHT** because of Trap's thunderous snoring, I was summoned by Robotix at the crack of dawn. It was time for the opening game against the **gelatinix** aliens!

Everyone was impatient to get on the field . . . except me!

Then I heard a familiar holler. It was Grandfather William, who looked **relaxed** and **REFRESHED** after a night in the fancy imperial suite on the 112th floor of the hotel.

"So, GRANDSON, ARE YOU READY? If you make me look foolish today, I may have to leave you on this planet!"

"O-of course, Grandfather!" I stammered.

At that moment, Sally's sweet voice cut in. "ADMIRAL STILTONIX, the captain has made great progress. I am sure he'll be fabumouse in today's game!"

Oh, Sally is such a fascinating mouse! Was she really talking about me? I guess there were no OTHER captains around . . .

I knew only one thing for sure — I absolutely COULDN'T let Sally down today!

As we approached the stadium, we began to hear a buzzing. It grew LOUDER and LOUDER and LOUDER, until we finally arrived inside the giant stadium. It was packed, and the fans were CHEERING like crazy!

46

Seven rings of seats **SURROUNDED** the field, and they were full of aliens of all kinds.

Benjamin hugged me **ENTHUSIASTICALLY**. "Wow!"

I swallowed—my throat suddenly felt drier than the **SAND** on the lunar desert. I hadn't realized that thousands of **eyes** (or even more than that, since some aliens each had a dozen eyes on their heads) would be watching us play! Walking out onto the field, I tried to concentrate on the **ONLY** eyes I cared about: Sally's!

Today's starting lineup included me, Sally, Benjamin, Lionel, the Tailtwister twins, and Whiskerkicks.

I was so deep in thought, I didn't realize that the game had begun and someone had passed me the ball! Before I could blink, an attacker for the GELATINIX team stole it out from under my paws and ran toward our goal, easily kicking it into the net.

I looked like such a FOOL — we hadn't even been playing for a minute!

Grandfather William yelled from the sidelines, "HEY, CHEESEBRAIN! WAKE UP!"

I knew I had to make up for my mistake. So

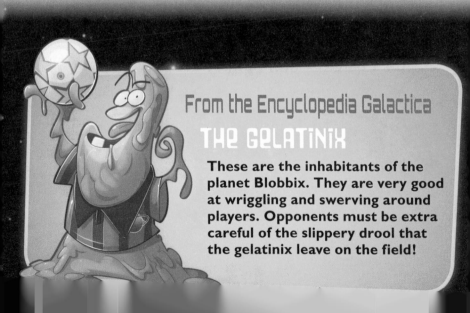

From the Encyclopedia Galactica
THE GELATINIX

These are the inhabitants of the planet Blobbix. They are very good at wriggling and swerving around players. Opponents must be extra careful of the slippery drool that the gelatinix leave on the field!

when the game started again, I sprinted up to the ball. But three **aliens** surrounded me immediately!

Panicked, I kicked the ball as hard as I could. The BALL took a funny bounce, but Sally headed it in the air and passed it to Lionel, who scored a tying goal! It was 1-1!

For the rest of the game, we were able to keep the score tied. During the last minute of play, Lionel darted forward, PLAYED the ball off an opponent's head, and used a super-turbo kick to score a galactic goal. It was 2-1!

The referee whistled to signal the end of the game. WE HAD WON!

Victory!

ADVENTURES IN
RECREATRON

After the game, our team decided to take a **walk** around Recreatron, the capital city of Athletica.

After a few minutes, we noticed that a group of ALIENS in the main square was pointing at us. One of them came up with a **STRANGE** device in his hand and spoke to me in an incomprehensible language.

"Sdhf bfh sgxrd asaainf djf?"

"Um . . . Robotix, can you translate?" I asked. My ears felt like they were stuffed with cheese!

"Of course, Captain!" Robotix replied. "It is Bobbonese, a spoken language—"

"Yes, yes, but what are they SAYING?" I interrupted. (When Robotix begins explaining something, he never stops!)

"The taller alien says that they are fans of SOCCERIX and would like to take a photologram of —"

A photologram? That is a special three-dimensional photograph that includes an autograph! No one had ever asked to take a photologram of *me* before!

I accepted enthusiastically. "Of course! Tell them yes!"

"But, Captain, they don't —"

I waved my paw. "Respond, Robotix! Let's not be rude!"

"GJTEVKF BJFJHK!" Robotix exclaimed.

I began to pose, ready for the photologram, but . . . HUH?

The alien who had spoken was headed toward *Lionel*!

The alien pressed a button, and the device let out a **BLUE RAY OF LIGHT**.

Bjfjk, Lionel!*

Lionel Ratessi

A moment later, a three-dimensional image of Lionel appeared in the air, with his autograph just below it.

Seeing my confused face, Robotix explained, "Captain, if you had let me **FINISH** translating, I would have explained that the alien wanted to take a photologram of Lionel Ratessi—not of you!"

*"Thanks, Lionel!"
in Bobbonese

I had made a stellar fool of myself . . . again!

I was about to say something when I spotted **two strange figures** out of the corner of my eye. I thought I had seen them before! Were they **SPYING** on us from the shadows?

A moment later, Benjamin called to me to keep walking. When I turned to look back, the figures had disappeared. Cheesy comets, what a **mystery**!

Huh?

Flying Rivals

The next day, we woke up full of ENERGY. When we arrived on the field for our game, we were ready to give it our all!

But then our opponents, the **WINGOIDS**, entered. They were huge, tall aliens—with WINGS!

"A-ARE W-WE SURE WE WANT TO PLAY?" I muttered to Trap. My whiskers were trembling with fright.

Trap rolled his eyes. "Geronimo, you're not scared of the wingoids, are you?"

Before I could reply, the whistle blew, and Trap ran toward the ball. The game had begun—I couldn't back out now! Today's starting lineup consisted of me,

Trap, Sally, Lionel, the Tailtwisters, and our goalie, Whiskerkicks.

I ran to the **middle** of the field, where Sally dribbled around a wingoid who was trying to STEAL the ball from her.

I gathered my courage and squeaked, "Sally, pass it to me!"

From the Encyclopedia Galactica

THE WINGOIDS

These inhabitants of the planet Featherflap are large, muscular aliens. Even if the rules of soccerix don't officially allow it, they always try to dribble the ball while flying!

Sally heard me and passed the **BALL** with an elegant move of her foot. I darted forward and yelled, "I've got it! I've got it! I've got iiiiit . . ."

I must have **MISCALCULATED**, though, because instead of kicking the ball, I **tripped** on it . . . and ended up sprawled out flat on the field like a Parmesan pancake.

While I was trying to get up, the largest

It's all yours!

I've got iiiiit!

SWOOOSH

wingoid player got control of the ball. With a quick flap of his wings, he took off, flying just above the field while keeping the ball on the ground. He ended up in front of our goal and was about to kick the ball into the net when the ROBOT-REF whistled. "Flying is not allowed on the field!"

HOLEY CRATERS! WE LUCKED OUT THAT TIME!

After that, Bugsy came into the game. She was able to QUICKLY slip past two opponents, make her way toward their goal, and pass the ball to Lionel. He wriggled between the legs of a wingoid and scored! It was 1–0!

The wingoids played hard, trying to tie things up, but we managed to keep them from scoring.

The game was almost over, and I was

SO TIRED. My legs felt like they were filled with moon rocks. Stumbling on my tired paws, I missed a pass. Oh no—a WINGOID got the ball and moved toward our goal!

When David Tailtwister got in his way, the WINGOID tried to scare him by suddenly opening his giant wings. But David wasn't intimidated. He blocked the shot!

A moment later, the robot-ref called the end of the game.

The SPACEMICE had won again!

"Tomorrow we'll play against the RUBBERLIANS. If we win, we'll be in the finals!" Lionel exclaimed.

The rubberlians were small, round, and seemingly HARMLESS aliens. I figured they wouldn't be hard to beat!

But oh, I was wrong . . .

WE'RE A TEAM!

When thinking about our next game, I hadn't accounted for the rubberlians' special skill: BOUNCING!

As soon as the robot-ref blew the whistle to start the game, some of the rubberlians changed shape. They tucked in their arms and legs and began to ROLL really fast down the field, passing the ball as they went!

Crusty space cheese—before I knew it,

From the Encyclopedia Galactica

THE RUBBERLIANS

These are the inhabitants of the planet Boing. They are soft, round aliens. On the soccerix field, they roll quickly from one corner to another, disorienting their opponents.

the rubberlians had scored two goals!

When our team gathered in the locker room during half time, we were all feeling DEJECTED.

"Uncle Geronimo, we're going to lose this time, aren't we?" Benjamin asked sadly.

I LOOKED AROUND at my teammates and thought about what to say. After the first two games, Soccerix didn't seem so bad. Actually, it was fun! Of course, it involved a lot of running, and facing **frightening** opponents, but I had learned something important — I could always count on my teammates to protect my fur.

Maybe it was time for the **TEAM CAPTAIN** to give a speech!

So I cleared my throat and said, "Yes, Benjamin, maybe we will lose. But that's not what's important! What's IMPORTANT is giving your all in the game and not forgetting that you aren't alone on the field. We can all count on one another, because we're a team!"

For once, Grandfather William nodded with satisfaction.

When the second half of the game began, we took the field like a different team. We were united and full of ENTHUSIASM!

And that's how we managed to score three goals: BUGSY made the first one by bumping the ball with her head, LIONEL made the second one with a kick over the heads of the defenders, and Benjamin slid the third goal around the goalie with some fancy footwork. We won 3–2!

No one could stop the spacemice!

A Queasy
Encounter

As we were celebrating our latest mouserific victory, my wrist phone rang. **Beep! Beeep! Beeeep!**

It was Thea calling from *MouseStar 1* to congratulate us and tell us that everyone on the ship had been watching the game. They were having an enormouse PARTY in our honor!

I was filled with pride. Now I couldn't wait to play in the final game!

As we LEFT the stadium, though, my happiness vanished like a cosmic cheese platter under Trap's snout. The ZOMBORGS—who we'd be facing in the final game—planted themselves in front of us threateningly.

Even though deep, deep down those creatures filled me with **fright**, I gathered my courage and stood up tall. "Hello, zomborgs," I said. "I am the **captain** of the spacemice, and —"

"I know who you are," one of the zomborgs interrupted me.

"Oh?" I asked, surprised. "Well, all right—good luck in the final! MAY THE BEST TEAM WIN!"

"You mean us, you *mousey microbes*," responded the biggest zomborg. Stellar Swiss, he almost knocked me out with his **PUTRID BREATH**! "It will be a horrible final for you!" he concluded. His friends burst out laughing as they all stormed off.

"What terrible creatures!" Sally commented, wrinkling her snout.

We can beat them!

And what **TERRIBLE** breath!

I sighed. "It won't be an easy game. Those aliens seem like they'll do whatever it takes to win."

"At least we have our secret weapon—Lionel!" said Trap with a grin.

Lionel proudly chimed in. "Those ALIENS don't scare me! They're big, but they're slow. If we can keep the ball close to the ground, I'm sure WE CAN BEAT THEM!"

Then Trap suggested, "Let's go into the city and celebrate today's victory! I spotted a place where they make excellent four-cheese shakes and—"

Grandfather William's voice stopped Trap midsentence. "No one is going anywhere, Grandson! Tomorrow morning we have to be up bright and early to TRAIN for the final game. So now it's time for all of you to get ready for bed!"

Oh, it was cosmically hard to be an athlete!

For a minute, I had forgotten that in order to win, we needed to practice!

A Missing Mouse

At eight o'clock the next morning, we all had to be out on the field, ready for our final day of practice.

The alarm clock **blared** in my ears. Cosmic cheese rinds! I leaped out of bed, but it was hard for me to stay on my paws—I had a terrible headache!

"I don't think that super-protein berry puree that Squizzy made us last night is agreeing with me," I said to Trap as he yawned and stretched. "My head is pounding!"

"I have a **GALACTIC HEADACHE**, too," he said with a groan. "It must be the stress of the final game."

We rushed to put on our **soccerix** uniforms and headed to the breakfast room. Squizzy, who could hardly keep

his **three eyes** open, was waiting for us with some algae. Yuck! What I wouldn't have given for a mozzarella milkshake!

A few minutes later, Benjamin arrived. "Good morning, Uncle. Ugh—I have an out-of-this-world headache this morning!" He looked around the room. "Is Lionel with you?"

I scratched my snout. "No . . . why?"

Benjamin **FROWNED**. "When I woke up, he wasn't in his bed."

"He must be around here somewhere," I said. "I'll call him!" I turned on my wrist phone.

Beep! Beeep! Beeeep!

No answer.

"Hmmm, he's not answering. Maybe he went for a walk. I'm sure he'll be back soon," I said, trying to reassure my nephew.

Before long, the rest of the team had **ARRIVED**, except for Lionel. Everyone had horrible headaches! We quietly ate breakfast together, but there was still no sign of **Lionel**.

Oh, for all the lunar cheese, where had he gone?

"Did he go back to the room? Maybe he had a headache, too," Bugsy suggested.

WORRIED, I accompanied her and Benjamin

to check the hotel room. Lionel wasn't there, but we did find his soccerix bag.

I tried to call him again. I heard the sound of a wrist phone: **Beep! Beeep! Beeeep!**

"It's coming from over here," said Benjamin, ducking down. "Lionel's wrist phone is **UNDER** the bed!"

Bugsy added, "And look! Some of **SQUIZZY'S** dried algae is on the floor. It leads to the window!"

We **noticed** that the window of the room was cracked open.

"Maybe someone *mousenapped* him!" Bugsy exclaimed.

Those words sent a **CHILL** down my back, all the way to the tip of my tail.

Lionel was in danger—and it was all my fault! I should have been keeping a closer eye on him. I felt like the **WORST** soccerix captain in history!

Just then, Sally arrived, and we filled her in. "Hmmm," she said. "There's even more algae outside. Maybe Lionel left it as a trail?"

"*Let's follow it!*" Benjamin proposed.

At that moment, my **phone** rang. Leaping light-years, it was Grandfather William!

"Grandson! You are late for practice!" he barked.

Hurry!

I didn't let him say anything else. "**GRANDFATHER, WE HAVE AN EMERGENCY!** Lionel is missing!"

"What?! This is unacceptable!" he hollered. "Start searching for him immediately!"

Grandfather was right. It was useless to stay where we were. We needed to **hurry** and find Lionel!

I **CRIED**, "Trap, Sally, come with me! Let's follow the **algae** trail!"

"We want to come, too," Benjamin and Bugsy pleaded.

I shook my head. "No, it could be dangerous! There's no telling what we're dealing with. You stay here in case Lionel comes back, and we'll keep in touch using our phones!"

LOOKING FOR LIONEL

The **algae trail** led into a forest of trees with violet-colored leaves.

"Are we sure that this is really **SQUIZZY'S** algae?" I asked, picking up some of the algae with my paw.

"Of course!" Trap looked at me, exasperated. "After eating this horrible stuff for two weeks, I would **recognize** it with my eyes closed!"

Suddenly, the algae trail stopped.

"Now what?" I asked.

"We need to look for **PRINTS**," responded Sally. "Like this one—**LOOK**!"

We all crept closer to what looked like

ZOMBORG footprints! We followed them silently, pushing leaves out of the way until we reached a clearing with a camper parked at the other end. Holey space cheese, could Lionel be in there?

We ducked behind a rock and watched the entrance to the camper carefully. Suddenly, two zomborgs came out, SNICKERING.

"We FOLLOWED those galactic goofs through the city for days, but it was worth it—we managed to CAPTURE that little rat before the final!" one of them said.

"KNOCKING THEM OUT with our breath was almost too easy!" the other one added. "Without their star player, beating them will be simple!"

His friend laughed. "HA, HA, HA! When we let him go, we will already be champions of the tournament!"

I was squeakless—that's why we all had headaches! The zomborgs had knocked us out with their toxic breath!

I turned to Trap and Sally and whispered, "We need to free Lionel—and to do it, we

We did it!

need to get those awful zomborgs **AWAY FROM THE CAMPER**!"

"Well, now that we don't have Lionel on our team, they'll be feeling STRONGER AND TOUGHER than us, right?" asked Trap. "So let's challenge them to prove it! Sally, come with me."

My fur stood on end. What was my crazy cousin planning?

I DIDN'T KNOW ... but I had a feeling that it might cause even more trouble!

A Fight to the Finish

Whistling absentmindedly, Trap sauntered up to the two **ZOMBORGS**. Sally walked just behind him.

"Hey there!" my cousin said with a friendly grin, waving to the aliens.

"What are you **SPACE RATS** doing here?" one of the zomborgs snapped.

"Oh, nothing!" Trap said innocently. "We were just taking a walk and thought, 'Why don't we go say hello to our opponents?'"

"We believe in good manners and fair play,"* Sally added. "After all, winning isn't

*The term *fair play* means that all athletes should exhibit fair behavior and respect for their opponents.

as important as playing and having a good time, right?"

The two zomborgs burst out laughing. "Ha, ha, ha! Good manners! Ho, ho, ho! Fair play! Hee, hee, hee! Funny!"

Just then, Brax (captain of the zomborg team) came out of the camper to see what all the noise was about. "Why are you laughing?" he asked his teammates.

Galactic Gouda! I thought. TROUBLE AHEAD!

After the two ZOMBORGS explained, Brax walked up to Trap and breathed in

Get lost, rat!

his snout. "Rat, we're **only** interested in winning—at all costs! Understand? Now get lost!"

"Understood!" Trap responded, trying to **hold his breath**. "You'll definitely win the cup tomorrow, anyway. Our **STAR FORWARD** left, so we have no hope! Your team is too strong —"

Brax interrupted, "Good! You understand. Now **SCRAM** before I really get angry!"

But of course Trap didn't leave. I didn't have a **cosmic clue** what he was doing!

Trap continued, "Since you're so much better than we are, how about you show us some of your skills?"

Brax snorted. "Don't worry! Tomorrow in the final you'll have a show you'll never forget! **Ha, Ha, Ha!**"

"So you don't want to show us now?" Trap

said **INNOCENTLY**. "Really? Or maybe it's because . . . you don't have any skills! Can you do this?"

Trap grabbed a nearby **SOCCERIX** ball and began to dribble it between his **feet**, then hit it with his head and his tail.

"Of course we can do that, rat!" Brax spat. "Rufus, show them!"

One zomborg copied Trap's moves.

Sally said indifferently, "Not bad . . . **but can you do this?**" She grabbed the ball and did a step over.*

DRIBBLE . . . .

STEP OVER

*A step over is a trick where a player spins her feet around the ball in order to disorient her opponent.

Brax was getting angry now. "**OF COURSE! TORX, SHOW THEM!**"

As one of the other zomborgs did the trick, more aliens came out of the camper, curious about the **unexpected contest**.

"Oh, cool," Trap said. "But let's see if you can do this!"

My cousin **PERFORMED** a sombrero*: He lifted the ball with his heel and kicked it over the head of one of the **ZOMBORGS**, then retrieved it from behind him.

SOMBRERO

*A sombrero is a trick where a player passes the ball to himself over the head of his opponent.

All the aliens let out a **gasp** of admiration, but they were immediately silenced by their captain.

"**That's easy!**" Brax scoffed.

As he tried to copy the tricky move, Sally turned toward me. She **WINKED** and pointed to the entrance of the camper.

Mousey meteorites—now I understood! Trap and Sally had gotten all the zomborgs out of the camper with their silly soccer challenge, and the coast was clear for me to FREE LiONEL!

RESCUE MISSION

I snuck out from behind the rock and slipped into the zomborgs' **camper**. There was no sign of Lionel near the door. I didn't see him in the main room, either.

I searched all the different rooms, but found nothing. Where had they hidden him?

I leaned against the wall to catch my breath. **Suddenly**, the wall moved, and I tumbled into a room of **STINKY SPACE TRASH**!

Martian mozzarella! I'd fallen pretty hard, so I checked my head, my paws, and my tail to make sure nothing was broken. Luckily, everything seemed to be in one piece.

Captain!

Behind me, I heard a familiar voice. "Captain!"

I turned and saw . . . Lionel! Our star forward was imprisoned in a soccerix net made of lasers! He whooped with joy upon seeing me, as if he had scored an amazing goal.

"I knew we would find you!" I exclaimed, turning the lasers off and freeing him. "Are you all right? Did they hurt you?"

Lionel shook his snout. "No, they didn't do anything to me!"

"Good!" I gave him a hug. That poor, brave mouselet had been through a lot. "Now let's get out of here. Trap and Sally are keeping the **ZOMBORGS** busy, but I don't know how much longer they can distract them."

We headed for the camper door—but then I heard a noise!

Cosmic cheese chunks, was it the zomborgs?

Then a familiar voice whispered, "Uncle, are you all right?"

I breathed a SIGH of relief. It was Benjamin and Bugsy!

"What are you two doing here?" I asked. "I told you to stay in your rooms!"

Uncle!

Huh?

Benjamin looked down at his paws. "I know, but we thought that you might **NEED** our help—and Grandfather said it was okay!"

"Come here," I said with a sigh, hugging them. "Now let's get out of here!"

We snuck out of the camper and hid behind the **ROCK** again, where I could see Trap and Sally busy performing a **tricky** acrobatic pass. I got their **ATTENTION** by waving a tree branch. As soon as he spotted me, Trap lost his **BALANCE**.

BONK
BONK
Bonk
BONK

He and Sally tumbled to the ground, and the zomborgs burst out laughing.

"Well, you won!" Trap told them. "You're just too good for us!"

"It will be a pleasure for us to lose the final game against champions like you," Sally added politely, waving and walking away.

"I see that you rats finally understand," Brax called after them with a sneer. "The pleasure will be all ours! Ha, ha, ha!"

MISSION ACCOMPLISHED!

GIVE IT
YOUR ALL!

A little while later, we arrived back at the HOTEL, where Grandfather William and the rest of the team was waiting. They were enormously happy to see us!

"Nice teamwork!" Grandfather said proudly, after we'd recapped our rescue mission.

"I'd love to see the expression on Brax's face when he discovers that LIONEL isn't there anymore," said Trap, laughing.

Grandfather clapped a paw on Trap's shoulder. "Good job, Grandson. It was a great idea to challenge those zomborgs to a SOCCERIX SHOWDOWN!"

Then he turned to me and said, "This time, I must admit, you were a little less of a **cosmic cheesebrain** than usual . . ."

Was Grandfather actually giving me a compliment? **I COULDN'T BELIEVE IT!**

He walked over to Lionel and patted him on the back. "Were you **SCARED**?"

You are a courageous little mouse!

Lionel shook his head. "No—I knew that my teammates wouldn't **abandon** me!"

Grandfather smiled. "And good thing they found you **RIGHT AWAY**, otherwise your mother would have turned us all into meteoric meatballs!"

We all burst out laughing!

Suddenly, Robotix began ringing like an alarm clock. "It's time for practice! TO THE FIELD! TO THE FIELD! TO THE FIEEEEEELD!"

Grandfather nodded firmly. "Robotix is right. Tomorrow is the final game, and we have to be our *best* against the zomborgs!"

We all put our paws together and cheered, "spacemice for one, spacemice for all!"

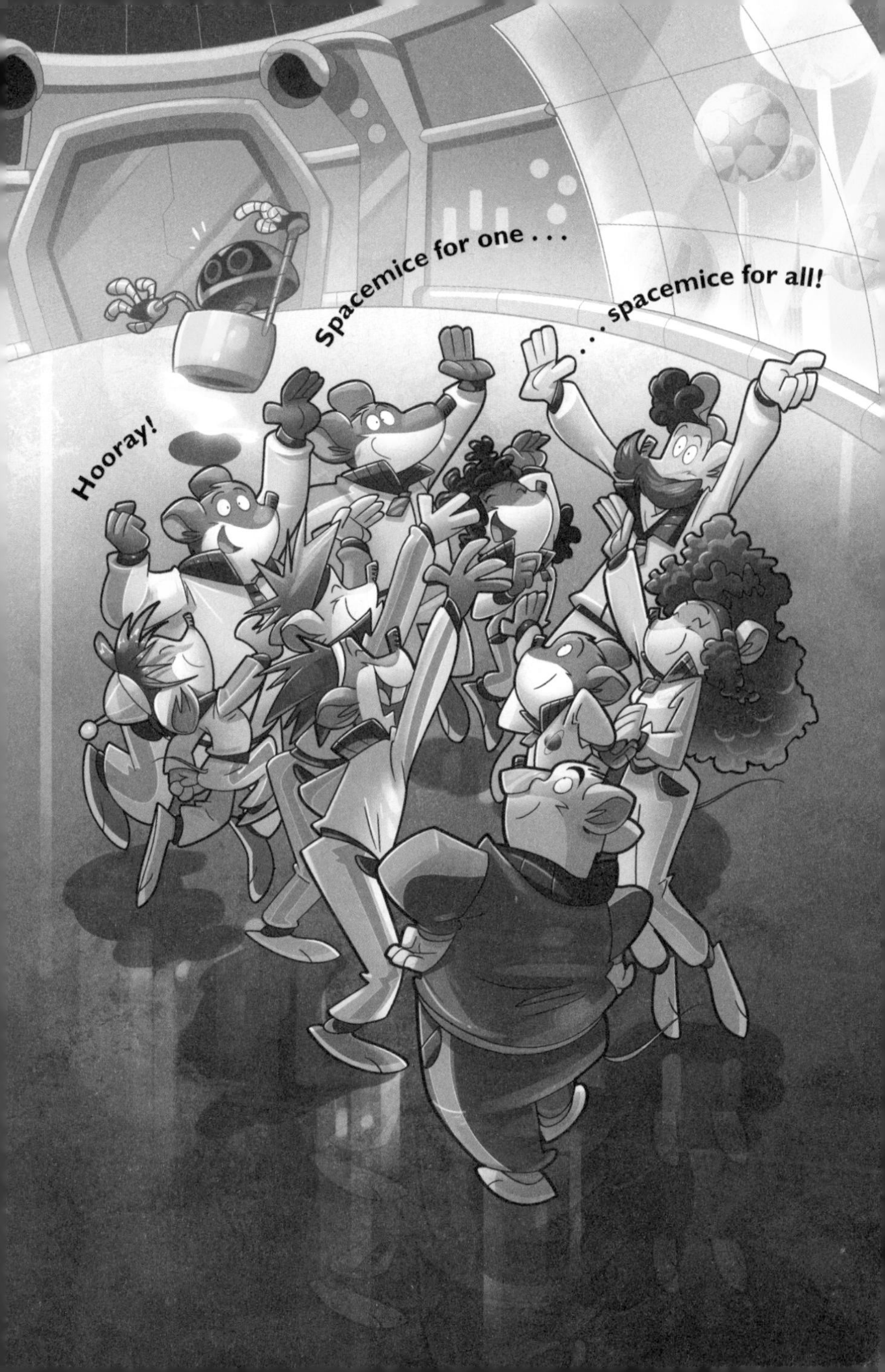
Hooray!
Spacemice for one . . .
. . . spacemice for all!

A MOUSERIFIC FINAL

The next day, I woke up with a fur-raising start! I'd had a **nightmare** that the zomborgs won the final game. As a prize, instead of the cup, they won the captain of the spacemice — **ME**! So I had to live on the planet Penaltex, which was covered with clouds of the same **noxious air** that comes out of the zomborgs' mouths. Galactic Gouda, that would be awful!

"Geronimo, what were you yelling about?" Trap asked, *rolling out* of bed.

"Uh, nothing," I mumbled. "I just had a nightmare!"

Trap grinned. "Huh. I dreamed that WE WON the tournament, and that the cup was made of cheese!"

I rolled my eyes. Trap was ALWAYS dreaming about cheese!

After breakfast and a warm-up practice, our whole team headed to the stadium. It was PACKED — there must have been thousands of spectators!

As we entered, Robotix explained, "All the galaxies are tuned in to today's game! It will be broadcast in UNIVERSALVISION!"

I gulped. We couldn't afford to make fools of ourselves today!

As we stepped onto the field, the zomborgs snarled at us.

Brax's eyes narrowed when he saw Lionel. He hissed, "Even if you've found your little rat, you have no CHANCE against us. We'll make you eat dust!"

Trap responded pleasantly, "Parmesan dust? Delicious, though I prefer slices if possible!"

Brax stomped away, snarling.

Before long, the robot-ref blew the whistle to start the game! Sally, Benjamin, Bugsy, Trap, Lionel, Whiskerkicks, and I all took the field.

For the first TEN MINUTES, we could barely touch the ball—the zomborgs kept getting in our way, pushing and TRIPPING us. But the robot-ref, with his infrared 360-degree vision, didn't miss a single foul. Three of the zomborgs were PENALIZED!

Eventually, Sally got the ball and freed herself from the tight defense of a zomborg, *slipping* away quickly.

She passed the ball to Bugsy, who immediately spun around and passed to Benjamin, successfully avoiding the alien defenders! My nephew was right in front of the ZOMBORG goal. Without pausing, he gave the ball an amazing kick . . .

GOOOOOOOOAAAAAAAL!

1-0 for the spacemice!

After our goal, the zomborgs were even more **aggressive**. Two of them began to run in front of the robot-ref to keep it from **SEEING** what was happening on the field!

Immediately, Brax took advantage of the situation and **BOLTED UP** to me, then pushed me down and stole the ball. He was

Move it!

right in front of our goal—and Whiskerkicks wasn't ready for him!

Just as Brax was about to KICK the ball into the goal, the two zomborgs moved away from the robot-ref. Now that the ref could see again, it watched the ball sail into the net. **RATS!** It was official—1-1!

Trap was furious. He waved a paw in Brax's face and yelled, "That's not fair! You're cheating!"

The **alien** began to laugh. "That's right, rat! This is how we have fun!"

The game started back up. We all played hard, but no one scored again . . .

With just a minute to go before the end of the game, Lionel got the BALL from Trap. He passed one zomborg, then a second one. Right as he was about to take a shot that would have been impossible to block . . .

BAM!

Brax tripped him, and Lionel fell flat on his snout, twisting his leg on the way!

TWEEEEEEEET!

Owww!

Brax was taken out of the game—and we got to take a penalty kick!*

This was our big moment. We could win the tournament, but our **BEST PLAYER** was on the ground with an injury!

The robot-medic examined Lionel and carried him off the field. Luckily, his injury was not serious. But we had a big problem: WHO WOULD KICK THE PENALTY SHOT?!

*A penalty kick is a direct free kick on the goal granted to a team when a foul is committed against them in their own penalty area.

KICK IT,
GERONIMO!

Starry space dust, taking a **PENALTY SHOT** in soccer during an intergalactic championship is no joke. I certainly had no intention of doing it!

But then Trap said, "You need to take it, Geronimo!"

"**M-m-me?**" I stammered. "But it's too important! I couldn't possibly —"

Sally jumped in, "You're our captain! You should take the penalty shot!"

Even Benjamin insisted, "Uncle, remember what I explained in practice—if you kick the BALL on the red dot, it's impossible to defend! You can do it!"

I DIDN'T KNOW IF I COULD DO IT, but I knew that a real captain had to be able to take charge. I guessed this was my moment to do that!

Gulp! I took a deep breath and stepped up to the ball. My whiskers were wobbling!

I stared down at the red dot that I was supposed to kick. Then I looked at the **ZOMBORG** goalie. He stood right in the center of the goal . . .

Tweeeeeeet!

Ack!

Galactic Gouda! I had to kick—and now! But I hadn't decided what side of the goal to aim for. **THE RIGHT? THE LEFT? OR MAYBE THE MIDDLE?**

I tried not to think too much. Instead, I ran up, closed my eyes, and **KICKED** the ball as hard as I could . . .

SWOOOOSH!

The ball transformed into a bright red streak. Like a *missile*, it flew into the goal! The zomborg goalie stood with his mouth hanging open in shock.

IT WAS A GALACTIC GOAL!

I had done it! I had hit the red dot and activated the super-turbo force!

WE HAD WON THE GAME!

THE WINNING GOAL!

1. I RAN UP . . .

TWEEEEEEEET

2. . . . KICKED THE BALL WITH MY EYES CLOSED . . .

3. . . . AND GOT A GALACTIC GOAL!

RAISE THE CUP, CAPTAIN!

Not surprisingly, the **ZOMBORGS** were terrible losers!

As we were leaving the field, Brax blocked my path and hissed in my face, "You won this time, **rat**, but we will meet again!"

I held my **breath** so I wouldn't faint from the *PUTRID STINK*. Then I responded cordially, "It will be our pleasure to play a rematch one day!"

We will meet again!

Brax stormed off with the other zomborgs, and we got ready to take the stage for the **AWARD CEREMONY**. Our snouts were projected on mega-screens around the stadium: spacemice in **Universalvision**!

Diego Goalor, president of the Intergalactic Federation of Soccerix, announced, "I declare the spacemice team the *intergalactic champions of soccerix!*"

The spectators roared as Diego handed me the Great Intergalactic Cup.

Everyone watched me as if I was supposed to do something with it . . . but what?

Grandfather bellowed, "Hey, Cheesebrain, *LIFT IT UP OVER YOUR HEAD*!"

I grinned. "Oh, right!"

As soon as I lifted the cup, FIREWORKS went off over the stadium! They made my fur stand on end.

In my **FRIGHT**, I lost my balance. The cup slipped from my paws and . . . oops! It fell right on the president's foot, making everyone around the **GALAXIES** laugh!

My snout turned red with embarrassment. Maybe it was time to **return** to *MouseStar 1* . . .

WELCOME BACK, CHAMPIONS!

Thea came in her ship to transport us to **MOUSESTAR 1**. As we were traveling, she said, "I imagine you must be tired, so I prepared your cabins for you and have given the orders for you not to be **disturbed** once you get home."

But as she spoke, it almost seemed like she was going to laugh. And was she WINKING at Grandfather William?

I shrugged and thanked her. I really couldn't wait to have a nice long **rest**!

When we arrived at *MouseStar 1*, we were ready to say good-bye to one another and head to our cabins when . . . the hangar door opened and a huge group of spacemice and aliens greeted us with **CHEERS** and applause!

Together, they all shouted, "Welcome back, champions!"

I looked at Thea in shock. She winked. She had prepared the surprise!

My rest and relaxation could wait. I joined the *festivities*. After all, it isn't every day that you get to be a **champion captain**!

Don't miss any adventures of the spacemice!

#1 Alien Escape

#2 You're Mine, Captain!

#3 Ice Planet Adventure

#4 The Galactic Goal

Up Next!

#5 Rescue Rebellion

Be sure to read all my fabumouse adventures!

#1 Lost Treasure of the Emerald Eye

#2 The Curse of the Cheese Pyramid

#3 Cat and Mouse in a Haunted House

#4 I'm Too Fond of My Fur!

#5 Four Mice Deep in the Jungle

#6 Paws Off, Cheddarface!

#7 Red Pizzas for a Blue Count

#8 Attack of the Bandit Cats

#9 A Fabumouse Vacation for Geronimo

#10 All Because of a Cup of Coffee

#11 It's Halloween, You 'Fraidy Mouse!

#12 Merry Christmas, Geronimo!

#13 The Phantom of the Subway

#14 The Temple of the Ruby of Fire

#15 The Mona Mousa Code

#16 A Cheese-Colored Camper

#17 Watch Your Whiskers, Stilton!

#18 Shipwreck on the Pirate Islands

#19 My Name Is Stilton, Geronimo Stilton

#20 Surf's Up, Geronimo!

#21 The Wild, Wild West

#22 The Secret of Cacklefur Castle

A Christmas Tale

#23 Valentine's Day Disaster

#24 Field Trip to Niagara Falls

#25 The Search for Sunken Treasure

#26 The Mummy with No Name

#27 The Christmas Toy Factory

#28 Wedding Crasher

#29 Down and Out Down Under

#30 The Mouse Island Marathon

#31 The Mysterious Cheese Thief

Christmas Catastrophe

#32 Valley of the Giant Skeletons

#33 Geronimo and the Gold Medal Mystery

#34 Geronimo Stilton, Secret Agent

#35 A Very Merry Christmas

#36 Geronimo's Valentine

#37 The Race Across America

#38 A Fabumouse School Adventure

#39 Singing Sensation

#40 The Karate Mouse

#41 Mighty Mount Kilimanjaro

#42 The Peculiar Pumpkin Thief

#43 I'm Not a Supermouse!

#44 The Giant
Diamond Robbery

#45 Save the White
Whale!

#46 The Haunted
Castle

#47 Run for the Hills,
Geronimo!

#48 The Mystery in
Venice

#49 The Way of
the Samurai

#50 This Hotel Is
Haunted!

#51 The Enormouse
Pearl Heist

#52 Mouse in Space!

#53 Rumble in
the Jungle

#54 Get into Gear,
Stilton!

#55 The Golden
Statue Plot

#56 Flight of the
Red Bandit

The Hunt for the
Golden Book

#57 The Stinky
Cheese Vacation

#58 The Super
Chef Contest

#59 Welcome to
Moldy Manor

The Hunt for the
Curious Cheese

#60 The Treasure of
Easter Island

#61 Mouse House
Hunter

*Don't miss
my journeys
through time!*

Meet
GERONIMO STILTONOOT

He is a cavemouse — Geronimo Stilton's ancient ancestor! He runs the stone newspaper in the prehistoric village of Old Mouse City. From dealing with dinosaurs to dodging meteorites, his life in the Stone Age is full of adventure!

#1 The Stone of Fire

#2 Watch Your Tail!

#3 Help, I'm in Hot Lava!

#4 The Fast and the Frozen

#5 The Great Mouse Race

#6 Don't Wake the Dinosaur!

#7 I'm a Scaredy-Mouse!

#8 Surfing for Secrets

#9 Get the Scoop, Geronimo!

Be sure to read all of our magical special edition adventures!

THE KINGDOM OF FANTASY

THE QUEST FOR PARADISE:
THE RETURN TO THE KINGDOM OF FANTASY

THE AMAZING VOYAGE:
THE THIRD ADVENTURE IN THE KINGDOM OF FANTASY

THE DRAGON PROPHECY:
THE FOURTH ADVENTURE IN THE KINGDOM OF FANTASY

THE VOLCANO OF FIRE:
THE FIFTH ADVENTURE IN THE KINGDOM OF FANTASY

THE SEARCH FOR TREASURE:
THE SIXTH ADVENTURE IN THE KINGDOM OF FANTASY

THE ENCHANTED CHARMS:
THE SEVENTH ADVENTURE IN THE KINGDOM OF FANTASY

THE PHOENIX OF DESTINY:
AN EPIC KINGDOM OF FANTASY ADVENTURE

THEA STILTON: THE JOURNEY TO ATLANTIS

THEA STILTON: THE SECRET OF THE FAIRIES

THEA STILTON: THE SECRET OF THE SNOW

THEA STILTON: THE CLOUD CASTLE

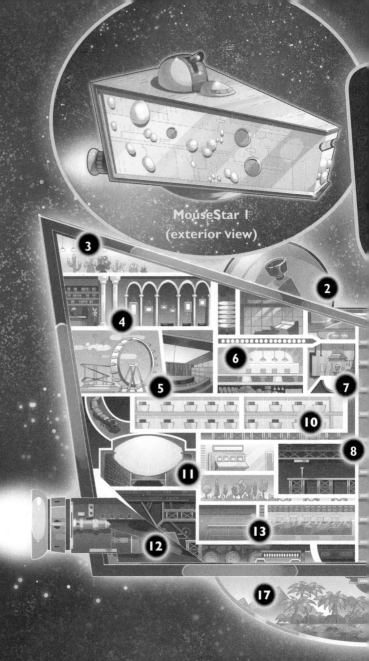

MouseStar 1

The spaceship, home, and refuge of the spacemice!

MouseStar 1
(exterior view)

Dear mouse friends,
thanks for reading,
and good-bye until the next book.
See you in outer space!